For Beginning Readers
Ages 6-8

This series of spooky stories has been created especially for beginning readers—children in first and second grades who are developing their reading skills.

How do these books help children learn to read?

- Kids love creepy stories and these stories are true page-turners (but never too scary).
- The sentences are short.
- The words are simple and repeated often in the story.
- The type is large with lots of room between words and lines.
- Full-color pictures on every page act as visual "clues" to help children figure out the words on the page.

Once children have read one story, they'll be asking for more!

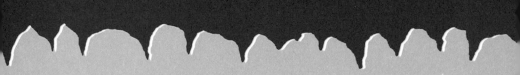
For Mom—J.D.

To Jesse, Maisie, and Adam...
and don't let the bedbugs bite!—A.W.

Library of Congress Cataloging-in-Publication Data

Dussling, Jennifer.
    Bug off! / by Jennifer Dussling ; illustrated by Amy Wummer.
        p.   cm. — (Eek! Stories to make you shriek)
    Summary: Bugsy, who delights in tormenting and destroying bugs,
finds out what it is like to be small, helpless, and a victim of
cruelty.
    [1. Insects—Fiction.   2. Behavior—Fiction.]   I. Wummer, Amy, ill.
II. Title.   III. Series.
PZ7.D943B1   1997   97-8785
[Fic]—dc21   CIP
                                                                         AC

ISBN 0-448-41726-X (GB)   A B C D E F G H I J
ISBN 0-448-41646-8 (pb)   A B C D E F G H I J

-to-Read
s 6–8

EEK!

Stories to make you shriek™

Bug Off!

By Jennifer Dussling

Illustrated by Amy Wummer

Grosset & Dunlap • New York

SQUISH!

Bugsy looked at the bottom

of his sneaker.

It was covered with bug guts.

He smiled.

"Ma! Bugsy is squishing bugs again!"

That was Mary Jane, his little sister.

What a brat!

She was always telling on him.

Someday he was going to

get back at her.

His ma came outside.

She had her hands on her hips.

"Billy, cut it out.

And Mary Jane,

don't call your brother that name.

Now go inside, both of you.

Play until bedtime."

Bugsy stomped up to his room.

He wanted to stay outside.

So many great bugs were there.

And Bugsy loved bugs.

He loved pulling off

their wings and feelers.

He loved sticking them with a pin

and watching them wiggle.

That was why kids called him Bugsy.

He sighed and looked

out the window.

Then he saw a bug on the sill.

It was gold with red zigzags

on its wings.

Wow! What a bug!

Bugsy flipped the bug over.

It rocked on its back.

All six legs waved in the air.

Bugsy laughed.

"Billy, time for bed!"

his mother called.

"In a minute, Ma,"

he called back.

"I'm playing."

Now the bug was trying to get away.

Bugsy flipped it over again.

OUCH!

The bug had stung him!

It felt like an electric shock.

A little drop of blood

welled up on his finger.

Bugsy was mad.

He was about to smash the bug.

But he stopped.

The bug was staring at him.

Little bolts of lightning

shot out from its feelers.

And there was a buzzing

in Bugsy's ears.

It almost sounded like words.

It sounded like someone saying,

"You will be sorry."

Then the bug flew

through a hole in the screen

and was gone.

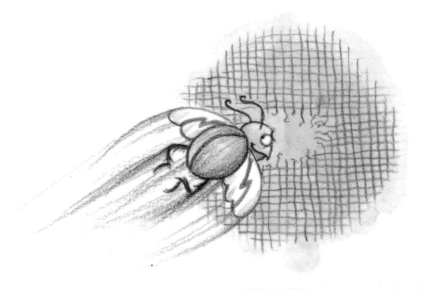

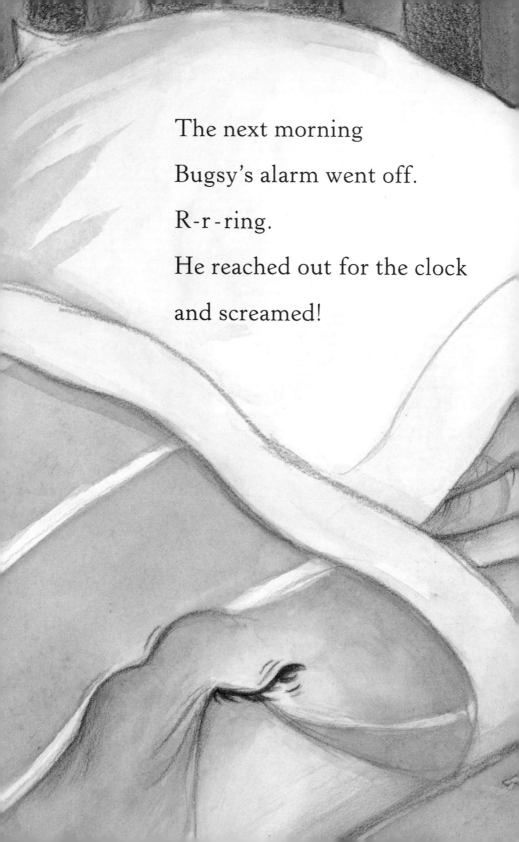

The next morning

Bugsy's alarm went off.

R-r-ring.

He reached out for the clock

and screamed!

His hand was gone.

And his arm was not an arm.

It was long and skinny

and black as coal.

It looked like a whip

or a piece of string…

or a bug's leg.

He touched his face.

His eyes felt like tennis balls.

His nose was gone.

Bugsy had gone to bed a boy.

He had woken up a bug.

But how?

It had to be that strange gold bug!

It had stung him.

It had said, "You will be sorry."

Was this what the bug meant?

Just then, he heard a noise.

"Time to get up, Billy!"

His ma!

His ma pulled back the cover.

Yikes! She was huge—

ten stories tall, at least.

She opened her giant mouth.

He saw her giant teeth.

"What is a bug doing in this bed?"

she boomed.

Bugsy watched her roll up

one of his comic books.

Oh no!

She was going to squish him!

He scrambled across the bed,

over the night table,

and onto the window.

In a minute
he was out the hole
in the screen.
He climbed down the side
of the house and
crawled into his backyard.

Bugsy took a look around.
The yard looked
very different.
He saw a broken shoelace.
It was as big as a garden hose.
Next to some flowers
was one of his toys.

It was a Dinobones figure.
It looked like something
from a monster movie.

Then Bugsy heard a noise.

It sounded like a rainstorm

or a waterfall.

He looked up.

It was Mary Jane!

She was squirting their puppy
with a hose.
Mary Jane was having fun.
The puppy was not.

Too bad Ma wasn't around.
Then she'd see
the <u>real</u> Mary Jane.

25

Now Bugsy heard another noise.

It sounded like a wave.

And it was.

A huge spray of water

from the hose shot out at him.

He ran.

But the wave got him.
Bugsy struck out wildly
with his legs.

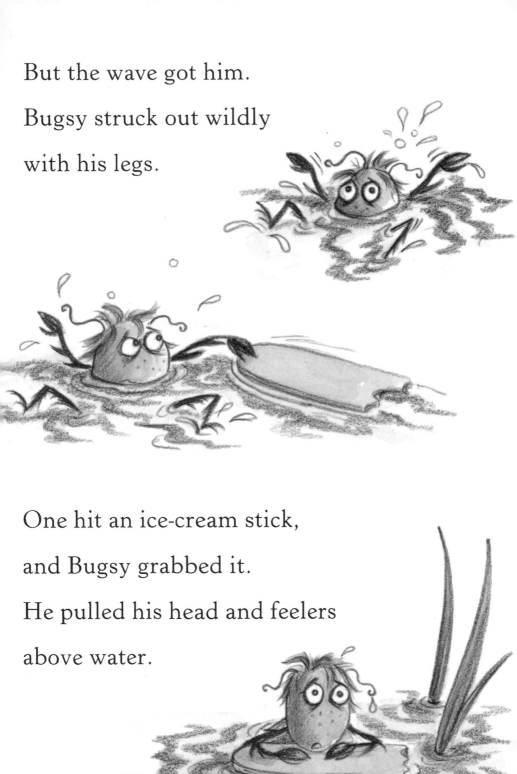

One hit an ice-cream stick,
and Bugsy grabbed it.
He pulled his head and feelers
above water.

Whew!

That was a close call.

Bugsy looked out

over the puddle.

How was he ever going
to get back to dry land?
He blinked his eyes.
Something was coming toward him.
It was the bug—
the gold bug!

The strange bug stopped
in front of Bugsy.

Little lightning bolts flew
between its feelers.

Bugsy could not look away.

"Sorry, yet?" it seemed to buzz.

Bugsy started to nod.

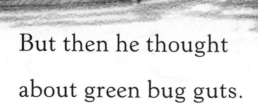

But then he thought
about green bug guts.

He <u>liked</u> squishing bugs.

And he was not sorry.

"No!" he yelled.

Then Bugsy wrapped

two skinny legs around the stick.

With all his might

he pulled himself up.

He paddled all the way to the grass.

Slowly he crossed the yard.

There were too many dangers outside.

Inside was safer.

He went past some flowers,

around an anthill,

and over a big gray rock.

Then on the porch he was blocked

by something shiny and black.

Bugsy knew what it was.

It was Mary Jane's shoe.

He looked up.

Mary Jane's foot was in the shoe.

She bent down to buckle it.

That's when she saw him.

"Oh, a bug!" her voice boomed.

"A nice fat bug!

And Bugsy is not around.

I guess I'll have to do the job for him."

35

She stood back up.

And then her shoe came down at him.

She was going to squish him!

Ooh, that Mary Jane!

Just wait!

Bugsy was going to get her back.

Somehow.

But right now he had to get away.

Fast!

Bugsy jumped and ran.

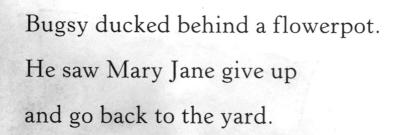

Bugsy ducked behind a flowerpot.

He saw Mary Jane give up

and go back to the yard.

But he did not see

the spider web next to him

until it was too late.

His right front leg was stuck in the web.

He tried to pull it off with another leg.

It got stuck too.

Bugsy wiggled and wiggled.

But he could not get free.

Soon he was hanging

upside down in the web.

The web started to shake a little.

Bugsy looked up.

A big fat spider

was walking across the web.

The spider clicked its jaws.

It was time for lunch!

The spider spun out some silk.

It wrapped up Bugsy

like a mummy!

Bugsy screamed.

The spider smiled.

Its skin started to shimmer.

Red lightning bolts

formed on its back.

And then the spider

turned into the gold bug!

"It's not nice to hurt bugs.

Is it?" buzzed the bug.

Bugsy's legs were pinned.

This was the end.

Bugsy cried out,

"No. It isn't nice.

I will never hurt

another bug again.

That's a promise!"

All of a sudden,

everything went dark.

There was a flash of lightning.

The next thing Bugsy knew,

the bug and the web were gone.

He was back to his real size!

Bugsy was a boy again!

From then on,

Bugsy never hurt or squished bugs.

And he told all his friends

to stay away from gold bugs.

There was only one person

he did not tell.

Mary Jane.